A Christmas Squirrel

Written by Mike Doodson • Illustrated by Ian Beck

A Christmas Squirrel is the winner of Amazon's
UK competition to find a reimagined version
of the festive classic *A Christmas Carol*.

"For Anais and Lauren"

It was Christmas Eve

and every creature and beast
was merrily busy, preparing a feast.
Woodland Hall was dressed with bright decorations,
ready for the next day's festive celebrations.

From the door wafted warmth and the sweet smell of spice,
among bunting strung up by a family of mice.
Here, each year the animals braved the cold weather,
celebrating and sharing their Christmas together.

A CHRISTMAS SQUIRREL

All except Squirrel,
who while out walking the wood
 had this magical time
quite misunderstood.
 You see, Squirrel cared only
for his own nut hoard,
 so the troubles of his neighbours
were always ignored.

A Christmas Squirrel

Pinned to the hall door
was a welcoming flyer:
   Join us for a feast and
a lovely log fire.
   Stocks are low - please bring
along whatever food is spare -
   we'll divide it all up and
each take a share.

"I've spent all year working
to build up my larder,
   maybe my neighbours
should have worked harder.
   I can't be expected to
share with them all."
   Squirrel said with a humph
as he passed Woodland Hall.

A CHRISTMAS SQUIRREL

There on the steps, with
their clothes full of holes,
  stood a poor, hungry family
of sad looking moles.
  "Forgive us. These few scraps
are all we could spare,
  we won't come tomorrow,
it wouldn't be fair."

"Nonsense," said Badger, "why,
you brought all you could,
  you're as welcome as
anyone else in this wood.
  Giving is hardest when
you've not much to give,
  there truly is nothing
for me to forgive."

A Christmas Squirrel

Back at his house, Squirrel checked up on his stores,
he had nuts by the shelfful, and more stuffed in drawers.
More pine nuts and hazels than a Squirrel could need,
but he still wanted more, such was his greed.

"Forget their party. With just one final forage,
I can start Christmas Day with festive nut porridge."
Squirrel knew where the very best nuts were kept,
so to his three favourite trees he scurried and leapt.

Squirrel stopped at the oldest pine in the wood,
he jumped as it spoke - he didn't know that they could!
"Squirrel, don't you know that an old pine tree like me
remembers exactly how it all used to be?"

Suddenly,

leaves rustled and rose from the ground,
  wrapping up Squirrel in a scene all around.
    It showed him his childhood and how he'd been caring,
      a kind and fun Squirrel, who also loved sharing.

The tree spoke once more, "See, you shared in the past,
all's not lost, you can still change if you're fast."
"A responsible Squirrel looks after himself,
and for me that means stockpiling nuts on my shelf."

A Christmas Squirrel

Squirrel felt sad upon seeing his youth,
  but he couldn't deny what he'd seen was the truth.
    "Enough," Squirrel thought. "Stop being so silly,
      there's still nuts to collect and it's getting chilly."

  Ignoring the pine, Squirrel pushed on with his task,
    but he didn't expect the next tree to ask:
  "Squirrel, don't you know that hazels note every deed?
  I've watched as you've collected much more than you need."

A Christmas Squirrel

"You're always asked to the feast but never attend,
 you're not a good neighbour and not a good friend.
  Why not share those nuts in which you take so much pride?"
   "But that's not fair. I found them all!" Squirrel replied.

   More leaves whipped up a vision, and Squirrel's eyes were glued.
  He saw creatures and their dusty shelves with next to no food.
 Squirrel felt uneasy and heard as he looked away,
"Stop them feeling hungry, share on Christmas Day."

Squirrel felt quite shaken up but made one final call,
 he hoped his favourite chestnut tree could make sense of it all.
  It wasn't unexpected when this tree raised his voice,
   "We trees can only show you, but you need to make the choice."

   "Squirrel, don't you know that a chestnut never lies?
  I show you now the future. See with your own eyes.
 If you continue hoarding all this food away,
you'll be alone in this wood come next Christmas Day."

A CHRISTMAS SQUIRREL

Then leaves once again arose,
swirled and filled the air
showing sad and hungry
creatures full of despair.
Squirrel saw the outcomes
his actions had brought,
for years he'd been greedy
without even a thought.

What use were the nuts
stacked up in their rows,
while others went hungry
right under his nose.
Feeling sorry, Squirrel raced
home determined to right
the wrongs of his past,
starting tonight.

A CHRISTMAS SQUIRREL

Christmas came and
Badger was first to the hall.
 He welcomed everybody,
"Merry Christmas one and all."
 Joining the party were
an owl, mice and voles,
 a red-breasted robin and
the family of moles.

Creatures came from far and
wide with spirits riding high,
 from rabbits in their warrens to
birds swooping from the sky.
 All sat down, with smiles spread
wide, full of Christmas cheer
 despite the fact the table
looked emptier this year.

A CHRISTMAS SQUIRREL

Then a thud
rattled the door, followed by a clatter.
   First the smell of food arrived, then Squirrel with a platter.
      "I've been a fool!" he shouted "Will you let me make amends?
         I want to share my food with you, my neighbours and my friends."

Squirrel brought out a plate of scrumptious hot food,
   as well as nuts he'd roasted, baked, fried and stewed.
   His piles of roasted chestnuts with caramel galore,
left spots of chewy stickiness on the wooden floor.

Squirrel said to Badger "It's almost hard to believe,
   I'm not the greedy Squirrel I was on Christmas Eve."
      Badger said, the hall so loud, by now he had to shout,
         "Giving and forgiving is what Christmas is about."

And with that, all in attendance raised up a Christmas toast,
   while Squirrel served up one huge smile and a stunning nut-filled roast.

Mike Doodson is a new dad and first-time children's author. He lives with his wife and daughter in Cheshire, UK.